Copyright © 2024 Michelle Burke
All rights reserved. No part of this book may be reproduced in any form without permission from the author or publisher, except as permitted by copyright law. To request permission, contact Author contact email
michelleburke@irishquill.com
edition number 2
Edition Published by Irish Quill
(Your Author Website)

"How do I start school Mum?" asked Fiadh. "You will see, my love. School is a wonderful place to learn and make new friends." Mum replied with a reassuring smile.

"How do I get ready for school in the morning, Mum?" Fiadh asked. "We will have a routine, brush your teeth, get dressed, eat breakfast, and then we will head to school together." Mum explained.

"What if I miss you, Mum?" Fiadh asked, her eyes filling with tears.
"You can think of me and know that I'm thinking of you too. We will see each other again after school and talk about your day."

"How do I know what to bring to school, Mum?" Fiadh asked. "Your teacher will give you a list of things to bring, and we will make sure you have everything you need." Mum said, smiling.

"What if I need to use the bathroom, Mum?" Fiadh asked, looking a bit worried. "There are bathrooms in the school, and you can ask your teacher anytime you need to go." Mum reassured her.

"What if I don't understand something, Mum?" Fiadh asked.
"It's okay to ask questions. Your teacher is there to help you learn and understand new things." Mum reassured her.

"What if I feel scared, Mum?" Fiadh asked, her voice trembling a bit. "It's normal to feel a little scared. Just remember, you are not alone. Your teacher and new friends are there with you." Mum said softly.

"Where do I put my things, Mum?" Fiadh asked, holding her new backpack.
"You will have a special hook in the classroom to keep your backpack and coat." Mum said.

"How do I know when it's time to go home. Mum?" Fiadh wondered. "Your teacher will tell you when the school day is over. and you will gather your things and I will be there to meet you.

"How do I do it, Mum?" Fiadh asked.
"You are a brave girl. Remember, everyone in your class is feeling the same way, you are all starting this adventure together." Mum said, waving goodbye.
Fiadh took a deep breath, smiled up at her mum, and stepped into the classroom, ready to start her first day of school.

The End